Philippe Dumas

CÆSAR

THE VILLAGE COCKEREL

J. M. Dent & Sons Ltd
London Toronto Melbourne

To Jean-Paul and Odile
whose hospitality is well known.

Translated by Deirdre Engel

Published in France under the title *César Le Coq du Village*
© Flammarion, 1978
First published in Great Britain 1979
English translation, © J.M. Dent & Sons Limited 1979
All rights reserved.
Made in Great Britain by
W.S. Cowell Ltd, Butter Market, Ipswich
for J.M. Dent & Sons Limited
Aldine House, Welbeck Street, London

British Library Cataloguing in Publication Data

Dumas, Philippe
    Caesar, the village cockerel.
    I. Title
843'.9'lJ   PZ7.D8935

ISBN 0-460-06963-2

My name is Caesar. If you happen to be passing by my village . . .

. . . stop in front
of the church
and look up . . .

4

. . . and you will see me perched up on top of the steeple.

And I also rather
enjoy being out in
the rain and hail.

I live up there because my job
is to tell which way the
wind is blowing.

However, last Easter,
I felt like going for a stroll
around the village.

Another thing I like
is having my head
in the clouds.

Luckily there was a thunderstorm
so I managed to leave my perch without
being seen.

I landed in the presbytery garden

I thought to myself: The parish priest must be a very kindhearted soul for he is always preaching about loving your neighbour.
But Lent was only jut over, and Heaven only knows what a clergyman's stomach is capable of after fasting for forty days.

I thought it unwise to carry on the conversation

Dugay the electrician was busy mending the oven and obviously had every intention of trying it out. I wasn't staying long there, either.

13

At the town hall, they clearly needed a cockerel to put up on their war memorial, which is what they do in France. That was no place for me either.

Old Dujardin was hoeing away in his kitchen garden. "There is your chicken pie, missus!" he shouted when he saw me.

Same problem at the *Bistrot de Paris* — the cook was only too happy
at the prospect of coq au vin for lunch . . .

When we reached Arsène's, I had hardly got inside the door when he came rushing at me brandishing his hand-saw. One look and I turned tail.

Thomas Quesnel put his foot down and came straight for me, the wretch!

Busard the farmer's son believed in the gentle touch, coaxing me with a "There, there, come along now, chick-chick" — all the better to wring my neck.

Etienne Dujour, whom I had always thought to be a peace-loving man like all cobblers, gave me a disappointing welcome: "Just you wait, you wretched bird or I'll bash your brains out with this hammer!"

Everyone in the village went for me with whatever they could lay hands on:
Rastiquet with a red-hot poker,

Albert with a great long needle,

Ma Pols with a five-kilogram weight,

Alphonse the baker with a two-pound loaf,

Hector with his butcher's knife,

Pignol the gendarme with his regulation pistol,

the man who cuts the grass on the side of the road with his scythe,

the bricklayer with his trowel,

the garage man with his spanner,

Madame Hélène with her scissors,

Jules the barber with what he had in his hand,

49

50   the man in the hardware shop who greeted me with an ominous smile . . .

the children who bombarded me with ink pellets . . .

Well, after all that, you would have done what I did in the circumstances, and, catching sight of my good friend the seagull . . .

. . . up I hopped and off we flew . . .

back to where I started from. What a relief it is to be way up here!
It'll be a long time before I go down there again.

56